Activity 1: Game

It was Friday. The beautiful, sophisticated and most well-heeled women in the City were prattling amongst themselves at a charity ball at an art museum, absent their powerful, businessmen husbands who usually accompanied them to such things. While they sipped champagne, and pretended to be experts on cancer, world hunger or whatever other cause their family's charitable foundations were championing, their husbands were off at their annual 'boys weekend' at the City Country Club. Cocktails, gossip and society magazine photo ops for the ladies. Golf, backroom politicking and brandy for the men. It was all a decidedly sexist affair, but it was a tradition amongst the City's elite power couples that continued with hardly any debate, lest they upset a social order that had allowed them to maintain their shiny images for generations.

However, the golf courses and parlors of the City's secluded country club were markedly quiet considering a group of fifty bombastic men were supposedly on holiday there. The wait staff idled in perfectly-pressed uniforms in these empty venues, not speaking a word of the oddity at the risk of offending the powers that be. All of the weekend's activities were taking place in a building at the edge of the club's grounds whose vaulted ceiling and old world architectural touches made it look more like a stately manor house than a modern pole barn.

Inside the large empty building bleachers had been erected facing a stage behind which was a white wall outlined in various colored lights. In the center of the wall was a mural, an artistic conglomeration of the world-famous logos of the various companies whose top executives were at the club for the weekend. On stage right was a glass and metal podium as modern as it was pretentious, with a small remote-control type device attached to its top. The stage was awash from array of ceiling lights and diffusers that would have rivaled a holiday movie set. And above the middle of the stage suspended from the ceiling by two massive metal beams, a strange contraption hung. It was a long box shaped object about the size of a refrigerator resting on its side, covered in a silky black cloth. Whatever the object was, it was humming slightly, barely perceptible in the empty auditorium.

Moments later, the businessman filed in coolly as if attending a board meeting. They were all dressed in tailored suits, some wearing jackets but most without, and were sharply groomed. Even the oldest of the group, a banker in his 60s, had the vigor and youthfulness of a man twenty-years his junior - the reward of a privileged, comfortable life. The men took their seats and a hush came over the crowd. The lights in the auditorium dimmed so that only the stage was lit, the lights along the wall began to flash in rhythm to thumping music. As the crowd began clapping in rhythm, the music got louder, the lights flashed faster and the lights shinnying down on the staged shuddered and flashed to add an air of almost game show excitement to the scene.

"Are you ready?" came a disembodied male voice.

"YES!" the men chanted in unison.

"I said are you ready?" the voice asked again.

3

"HELL YES!"

"Let's play!" the announcer said waving as he emerged as if from nowhere and took his spot behind the podium.

The announcer was a middle-aged, well-dressed man with slicked black hair and was holding a stack of note cards the backs of which all had the same amalgamated logo that was over the stage. He had a toothy grin and exuded charm like a professional TV game show host, pointing to various executives in the gathered crowd to greet them by name. When the crowd quieted down again, the stage lights dimmed, the music faded out and a spotlight shone on the announcer.

"Gentleman, welcome to the Annual City Club Rupture Fest!"

The crowd went into hysterical cheers, an older weapons-contractor executive in the front row threw his tie and jokingly cat called "We love you!" to the announcer. The music briefly roused before fading again, and the audience quieted back down, leaning in as if hung on the announcers every word.

"I'm Jack and I'm glad to be your host again this year. We have a busy agenda as you saw in invite letters you all received, and a lot more events so fella's this is gonna' be the only time all of you are at the same event until the banquet Sunday night."

The sound of paper shuffling could be heard as men pulled out the invitations Jack had alluded to and briefly glanced over the itinerary. Friday, Saturday and Sunday were each broken into three sections 'Morning', 'Afternoon' and 'Evening'. Friday's 'morning' slot was marked simply 'Arrival, guests settling into their rooms', and Friday afternoon was marked 'The Game Show', its font red to indicate that it was new for this year. The executives had already RSVP'd in advance which events throughout the weekend they wanted to attend. Friday evening had three listed events -- 'Market Mash Up', 'Darts and 'Power Grab'. No further explanatory text or information was given as if the attendees already had long-standing knowledge of what these events were... Saturday and Sunday's three slots each listed three more events each with names such as "Intern Interview" and "Golf", but Sunday evening only listed one event "The Banquet". After a few moments, and some excited whispering amongst themselves, the men put their programs away and turned their attention back to the stage.

Jack continued, "You're probably all wondering what The Game show is this year. It's not as hands on as 'Power Grab'..."

A few of the executive chuckled knowingly.

"But we're sure you're going to like it. Let's just give the boys a few minutes to get everything setup."

While Jack made chit chat and poked playful fun at the executives, strikingly-efficient men dressed entirely in black and wearing mirror-like sunglasses were busily setting up the stage of the 'game show'. Two waist-high white tables, supported by only one slightly curved, elegant leg that seemed ostensibly insufficient to hold the table top's weight were put on the stage a few feet from each other. On the table tops, as could been seen more clearly by the executives on the higher tier seats, were red circles at the middle. Behind the table, a sleek white pole at least eight feet tall was erected, each bolted to the ground and tested for strength by being shoved and pushed on by three of the men in black at once. Meanwhile, the shroud was removed from the object suspended over the stage, and a man in black seemed to take a quick measurement to verify that the tables were positioned equally under the thing. Compared to the sleekness of the rest of the stage props, the box over the stage was an unpolished mess of visible gears and pulleys. Audible murmurs of confusion filled the crowd.

Finally, the last man in black to leave the stage, stopped, turned around and reached into his pocket for something. He placed two large walnuts - one each - inside the red circles on the tables, looked up one last time to verify everything was in position, then left the stage.

"Here's how the game works,"

Jack pressed a button on the podium and two black chains slowly descended from the box toward the tables.

At the end of the chains were small black weights, about the size of a grapefruit, and perfectly round. There was no indication of how much the balls weighed, but given the elaborate contraption needed to keep it and the chains aloft it could be concluded that it was heavier than they appeared. The chains descended until the weights touched the walnuts slightly, then - without any input from Jack's control panel the chains retracted slightly until the weight was just barely touching the top of each nut.

Jack continued "In a moment we're going to bring out two of the boys your companies so graciously volunteered and set them so that their family jewels are on the table like these walnuts. Then I'm going to ask each of them a series of trivia questions, some hard some easy."

The crowd nodded.

"If he gets it wrong, this happens..." Jack pushed a button. The contraption holding up the chain made an odd series of clicking sounds but nothing appeared to happen; the crowd's confusion was palpable.

"And if he gets it right, this happens..." jack pushed another button. The chain above the left table rose slightly.

"The object is to answer as many questions right as you can..." Jack pressed a button multiple times until the chain above the left table was nearly twenty feet in the air - the chain nearly totally retracted back into the mechanism.

"That way you place your opponent in the most peril if his weight were to, say... drop."

A chuckle erupted from the crowd.

"However, if you get cocky and the other player starts answering questions right too..." Jack pressed some buttons and the chain over the right table rose until the weight was five feet above that table's walnut.

"And if you get nervous and start answering questions wrong." Jack pressed another button. The strange clicking sound filled the theatre until the chain above the right table quite suddenly was released, sending the weight crashing onto the walnut cracking it in two.

"You see, when a player answers a question wrong, the mechanism holding his chain is loosened until... well you see what happens. So the object of the game is to answer as many answers right as you can to make sure opponent's nuts are in the most danger. Oh, and to make it more interesting, the higher the weight goes for a player, the harder his questions become making it more and more likely that he'll answer wrong and..." Jack smiled wickedly as he pressed another button on his control panel.

The weight above the left table was released, the weight fell from nearly twenty feet, colliding with the walnut below so hard fragments of shell hit some of the men watching in the front row.

The crowd erupted into cheers. This was going to be a fun game.

The men in black brought out two strapping, naked young men, and tied their hands and feet behind the poles at the tables, holding them firmly in place. They then proceeded to roughly grab and tug out each set of balls, binding their sacks with athletic tape until the contents of each sack bulged obscenely, pulled several inches from their bodies, the skin so taught on each set that it seemed to shine.

Each set of nuts was then placed inside the red circle on their respective table and held in place by an upside down U-shaped clamp. Each young man struggled and tugged, but their balls were totally trapped, inside the strike zone of the hanging weights. Meanwhile, above, the contraption was making all manner of noise as the chains and weights reset. The chains slowly descended until the weight contacted each pair of balls, like it did with the walnuts.

"So, let's meet our players, Rob and Trevor, graciously um... donated, by the ninety-nine percent."

The gathered executives erupted into laughter, as if totally undisturbed at the macabre nature of Jack's statement.

Rob, a tall pale skinned lad couldn't have been more than 25. He had an average build, no strongly-defined muscles, but not quite flabby either. He had dusty brown hair that partly covered his eyebrows and boyishly handsome looks. To this right was Trevor, shorter than Rob by a good twelve inches, but in superior physical condition. His Latin complexion glistened under the studio lights. His pectoral muscles where perfectly chiseled, his legs powerful and well defined and his arms, even taught from being pulled behind his back, were rippling with muscles.

Each 'contestant' had amply large nuts, Rob's coming in slightly larger, but each testicle the size of small eggs. Trevor's were more round, Rob's, more oblong, but both were at serious risk of being neither large nor round...

Jack dramatically cleared his throat and started the game "Let's begin!"

A dramatic orchestral strike filled the auditorium, the spot light lifted from the announcer's podium and focused instead on Rob and Trevor. The intensity of the lights was already causing the two to sweat.

The sight of the two helpless handsome lads -- one an 'every man', the other a hunky 'alpha jock' being held captive, knowing that at any moment all signs of their masculinity could be turned into goo, was too much for some in the audience. The sound of multiple zippers being unzipped filled the air as some of the men began pulling out their own tools to play with while they watched.

"Question one goes to Trevor. What color is a red fire truck."

"Red! Please let us go..."

"Correct!" Jack pushed a button and the chain above Rob's bulging sack rose slightly.

"Question two, Rob. What color is a blueberry?"

"Blue! Please..."

The chain above Trevor's huge nuts rose.

The crowd erupted into laughter at the boys' plight.

"We just wanted to test out everything, and make sure each guy is at least in a little danger! Now to the real questions..."

Trevor and Rob each answered their respective next two questions correctly, making each weight about five feet above the doomed sacks. After answering each one correctly, the men would give the other a sidelong pleading glance as if to say "I'm sorry I'm pretty much guaranteeing your nuts are toast by answering this question right."

It was now the seventh overall question, and Trevor's fourth. He glanced up nervously, by now sweat profusely dripping from his forehead, and watched the weight dangling over his bloated Latin baby makers, waiting for its moment to squash them to mush.

"Question 7, Trevor. What element discovered in 1950 is named after the most populous U.S state?"

A hush gathered over the crowd, some of the men leaned forward in breathless anticipation that Trevor would answer incorrectly and in turn crush his balls. Up to that point the questions had been getting harder but were still within the realm of common knowledge. Not anymore.

"Um..."

"Clock is ticking..." Jack laughed, his hand hovering dangerously close to Trevor's penalty button.

"Californium. It's Californium."

"Correct!" there was a cranking of gears and the ball waiting to scramble Rob's eggs rose ever higher. A portion of the crowd erupted into cheers, with those who were eager to see Rob's skater boy nuts turned to peanut butter approving of Trevor's right answer.

"Now Rob, we always see the same side of the moon. Why is that?"

A hush befell the audience.

"Um... gravity?"

Jack paused, and placed his hand over his right ear as if listening to a hidden speaker there.

"That is incorrect. We were looking for tidal locking. Tidal locking is the answer."

The crowd gasped as a grinding of gears indicated that the mechanism holding up Rob's weight was loosening...

"Okay, looks like you're safe for another round. Next question for Trevor.

The announcer went on to ask Trevor a surprisingly convoluted question about some obscure accounting rule. Many in the audience assumed the street-smart stud would get it wrong and there was a collective audible gasp when the announcer declared.

"Correct!"

The weight above Rob's sack rose ever higher. It was not nearly to the ceiling. There wouldn't be anything left of his nuts if it fell now...

"Okay Rob"

Rob, clearly flustered, was more concentrated on the weight than getting the question he had just been given right. He responded in a rush, realizing he was wrong before the buzzer had even gone off. The gears cranked and ground, but nothing happened. The announcer had just turned to ask Trevor the next question when....

"It's dropping!" someone in the first row screamed in giddy excitement.

Rob looked up as the heavy weight fell from the sky toward his nuts. He screamed, begged struggled, and the weight fell as if in slow motion, mocking the end of his manhood.

The weight dropped lower and lower, picking up speed as it fell until...

SPLOOOSH!

The weight collided with Rob's nuts and didn't even slow down until it hit the table top with a wet thud. Rob's nuts did not gradually compress upon impact, they exploded instantly into chunks that showered the audience as if two fleshy cherry bombs had popped. The men in the first two rows were covered with nut meat, which had been turned to chunks of goo. Rob's pent up sperm and pieces of liquefied ball gunk splashed the back row. Rob's eyes were locked in horrified gaze at the weight resting on a pile of gooey mess that once been his huge, firm balls. There was simply nothing left of them now, except the splattered nut goo that was now being wiped off the faces of the City's elite businessmen.

"Well, I guess Trevor is the winner!" the announcer said coolly and dramatic music began to play over flashing lights.

By now Rob was in hysterics as the well-rehearsed men in black swooped the stage to clean up the mess. Trevor was roughly freed from his constraints and lead off stage. Meanwhile, one of the men lifted the heavy ball weight from Rob's totally deflated sack, dropping it nearly on his foot it was so slick with ball guts. The audience laughed.

Without being prompted a few of the men came to the stage to examine the damage up close. Rob was comatose, freed from his constraints, his limp body being held up by a man in black.

"They're totally flattened," one of the businessmen said grabbing the totally squashed sack in his hands, its mushed contents had been completely squeezed out like a burst sausage.

"I can't believe it! There's nothing left!"

"Just mush"

The men continued to fondle the ruined equipment, totally amazed at how absolute the destruction was. The gooey mess hardly even resembled balls.

"Gentleman, gentleman. This is just a taste of the weekend to come!"

The crowd cheered as the ruined skater was lifted and carried off stage. As they dispersed, a middle age executive named Greg Robins was tapped on the shoulder,

"So, Robins, where are you headed this evening?" asked a wide-eyed man in his fifties, a bit of Rob's goop still visible on his forehead.

Greg smiled, "Market Mashup sounded fun. I heard they totally changed it up this year,"

"I would hope so, that damn whack-a-mole mallet thing was so hard to use last year,"

Greg laughed.

This was gearing up to be the best Rupture Fest ever... and it was only the first day.

Activity 2: Market Mashup

The fifty businessmen who had gathered for Rupture Fest had broken into smaller groups of sixteen or so for the next activities. Greg Robins, a financial executive in his late thirties with neatly styled black hair, was standing with fifteen other men in a small room, four posts protruded from the ground along the back wall. At the front of the room one of the hosts, a friendly looking young man in his early twenties and dressed entirely in black, was explaining the rules of the game called Market Mash Up.

"Welcome to Market Mash Up, gentleman. I see a lot of familiar faces but a few of you are new so let me just go over this activity,"

As he was speaking, his voice cool and professional, his audience clad in their finest attire as if preparing for a power lunch, no one seemed phased as a door on the side of the room opened and a line of four young men, gagged and with hands bound behind their backs, was lead in. Each young man was being led into position by one of the events ubiquitous, ruthlessly efficient men in black, mysterious, relatively short men dressed in black suits and black sunglasses who - while never appearing to speak or signal to each other - executed all event's setups flawlessly.

"Each of you signed up for this event after last year's Rupture Fest and we've been tracking the stock performance of your companies since then to see who had the largest gains..."

The host continued calming talking as the struggling young men were each placed against one of the posts along the room, their arms and hands secured behind their backs and their legs spread apart by a metal bar at the ankles. Each was naked, and all were sporting -- as was a specific requirement to be involved -- massive sets of nuts. The men were gagged and their restraints given a final inspection by the men in black, who stepped away from and to the side of each, as if guarding against the unlikely event of an escape.

The first young man was an athletic, tall blonde with powerful legs, a broad chest and ample dangling nuts. The next was a muscular Latino man in his early thirties with scruffy facial hair and truly donkey sized nuts between his tree trunk legs, bulging invitingly in a tight, unyielding sack. The Latin's sack was so stuffed, his scrotum glistened from being so taught. To his side was a skinny, lanky skater type in his late teens with jet black hair and a pair of modest nuts that hung down a ridiculous, almost comical distance from his body. And lastly there was a bear-cub, scruffy man in his early thirties with fiery red hair, a mustache, huge broad shoulders and arms and huge, oval shaped nuts protruding from his fire red crotch.

"Well the results are in... having gained the most for the year the representative from Omnicorp gets to be this year's masher! Congratulations, Greg Robins!'

The crowd of men applauded wildly, patting Greg on the back as he made his way toward the host.

"Thank you! This is gonna' be a blast."

RUPTURED

Greg's Armani slacks strained to contain his growing erection. He had participated in Rupture Fest for three years now and had never been able to personally rupture any of the donkey-balled studs he'd watched get nutted in increasingly creative and splattering ways. This was the chance of a lifetime.

"Now, in the past for Market Mash Up we let the winning executive nut four guys for our amusement using this old-fashioned thing," the host held up a heavy, metal mallet and flung it indifferently toward one of the bound young men, the mallet bouncing off his thigh.

"But our friends over at weapons contractor Consolidated Iridium AG have let us try out this..."

The host help up a gray, somewhat bulky glove. The audience's confusion was apparent.

"Anyone ever seen Iron Man? Well this is a real-life exoskeleton - like that movie - there are servos and gyros and lord knows what else..."

"All soon-to-be available from Consolidated Iridium," a white-haired executive in the crowd - presumably a senior player at the company - interjected to polite chuckles from his colleagues.

"The workings are straight forward, whatever force you exert, will be amplified by the glove. Let me show you,"

The host slipped on the glow and tapped it rapidly with his other hand, there was a whirring sound as the glove came to life. He motioned for one of the men in black to bring him something, which turned out to be a walnut.

He took the nut in his ungloved hand and squeezed futility as the rigid object barely noticed. Then he put it in his gloved hand and, with the slightest effort, crushed the nut to powder.

The men all laughed, eying the captives hungrily, eying the balls they knew were about to face the same fate. The captive's eyes bugged out and all four began to squirm wildly, trying to protect their nuts.

"So, Mr. Robins, I present to you the Inifitrex 76-G, the combat glove for the next generation of soldiers.

Greg took the glove from the host and put it on. It wasn't as bulky in feeling as it looked, but was much heavier than he expected considering it appeared to weight as much as a normal leather glove. Greg took a few minutes to flex his fingers and get a feel for the glove, making sure to squeeze and punch the air while making eye contact with each captive, as if to say "kiss your sack goodbye."

The gathered executives were eager to see just how much damage this glove would do to the eight baby makers on display.

"Let's start with you, blondie." Greg walked up to the blonde kid and gave his nuts a playful squeeze with his ungloved hand. The blonde pleaded and struggled.

The blonde's nuts were about the size of large walnuts -- a perfect size considering the earlier demonstration -- and hung loosely in their sack. The left hung slightly lower, and was more oblong, so Greg decided to focus on that one first.

Greg reached out, positioning the dangling left nut between his thumb and forefinger and began to squeeze. Through the glove, he could feel the warm, pulsing organ being squeezed between his fingers. It was almost perfectly round, firm to the touch and... SQUISH! To Greg's surprise, his thumb and forefinger were now virtually touching, separated only by a thin piece of scrotum.

The young stud screamed hysterically through his gag and his legs convulsed wildly attempting to protect his manhood. Although Greg thought he was only barely touching the boy's nuts, the added strength provided by the glove proved otherwise. He opened his finger and observed his handy work. The left nut had been totally blown apart, crushed effortlessly by only two fingers. Greg grinned.

"Ooops!" he said mockingly to the crowd's delight.

He reached for the right nut and again trapped it between his thumb and finger. Not wanting the end to come quite so quickly, or unexpectedly less he miss the sensation, he was mindful to close his fingers slowly. He met eyes with the quivering stud and he felt in detail the membranes and tissues of the doomed nut crumpling and exploding until again his thumb and finger were touching. The whole thing took less than a few seconds, but to the trapped young man it felt like a thousand years. His eyes shot open in bright panic, then his head went limp. He was out.

"This thing is great!" Greg said grinding this thumb and finger together, feeling the already cracked nut being turned into paste inside the sack. "Whose next!"

"Pop the Latin kid!"

"Crush the skater!"

Greg stepped back from the comatose blonde and eyed the remaining three men. He was incredibly aroused by the power this seemingly incurious glove gave him over the six ample baby makers before him. He paced back and forth, making telling gestures such as clenching his hand and making fists which he fired into the air -- a hit that would almost certainly destroy a pair of genitals. He eyed each man, licking his lips and imagining the best way to wreck someone's sex life.

"Let's pop these balloons" he said laughing as he stopped in front of the taller, lanky skater.

The young man was trembling, tears streaming from his eyes. He knew he only had mere moments to remain a full man.

"Hmm how should be burst these bad boys?"

The crowd went wild calling out suggestions. Punching them, squeezing them. Ripping them off.

"Ah, I know, these things are already hanging so low, I might as well get in some sparring practice."

The skater's eyes shot open in sheer terror and he screamed uncontrollably into his gag. Greg, ignoring the muffled pleas for mercy, knelt so that he was at eye level with the skater boy's large, swinging nut sack. The skater's nuts were big and were by far the lowest hanging. They swung nearly six inches in the loose, hanging bag, resting at the bottom like two fleshy eggs. Greg balled his gloved hand into a fist and positioned the knuckle directly at the seam of the boy's sack, he wanted to make sure his aim was dead on.

"Count down with me!" he encouraged the crowd as he began moving his fist away from the swinging targets.

"Five... four.... three..."

Greg's fist was as far back as it would go, as if such preparation was hardly necessary considering the glove could likely have cracked his nuts with the equivalent effort of a light slap, but Greg wanted to be especially sure these nuts were mushed. The boy was writhing and screaming, his nut sack bouncing from the movement but still in harm's way. The excitement in the room was palpable. Would the boy's nuts be mushed totally in the sack on impact? Would the sack split open? Would the dangling sack be knocked clear off like a sparring target hit off its supports?

"... two... one!"

There was an audible whoosh as Greg's fist sailed through the air, followed by a satisfying, echoing wet splat. Greg's fist collided full force with the swinging sack which promptly exploded open like a piñata. Since the brunt of the force was directly between the trapped nuts, the outward force forced each nut -- each instantly turned to goo on impact -- to explode out of the left and right sides. the nut goop sprayed out in both directions for several feet, and Greg's cock twitched in his dress pants as he replayed the feeling of so viciously snuffing out any hope skater boy would ever have kids. Skater boy's head instantly rolled to the side and he was out, the liquefied remains of his nuts now dripping out of the holes in his sack.

And then there were four nuts.

"Latin boy next!" Greg shouted to the crowd's approval as he sprung to his feel and stood face to face with the Latino captive. Although he had tried to remain defiantly stoic through the affair, watching two sets of huge, proud nuts be annihilated in a matter of seconds had turned the Latin stud into a quivering mess as it became clear that he would never be able to spew any of his rich, creamy salsa.

"Please! Don't!" the young man screamed, muffled unintelligibly by the gag.

Ignoring him, Greg reached down until he could feel the warm, throbbing balls in his fist. By now, Greg was getting the hang of the glove so could cradle the Latin's donkey balls in his fist without instantly crushing them like he had done to the blonde. The two made eye contact for what - to the Latin - seemed to be a long time. His pleading eyes ostensibly having no effect on Greg.

"Ya' know what guys," Greg started, not taking his eyes off his victim.

"I think these balls might be too nice to just be burst open, at least not yet."

As he spoke, Greg bounced the balls in his fist, squeezing them and sizing them up. They were by far the largest in the room and firm. They were tight in their sack, so bulged invitingly, especially with the added pressure from Greg's gloved hand. In different circumstances, Greg would have been on his knees licking and sucking such beautiful baby makers, but this was Rupture Fest and popping them would be much more fun, Greg concluded.

"Why don't we give this guy a break..."

SPLOSH! CRUNCH!

"... or not!"

The Latin stud, who had believed he was going to be shown mercy, opened his eyes wide and screamed in genuine surprise and horror. He looked down to see that his liquefied nuts had exploded in the now clenched fist, Latin sperm and nut gunk oozing from between Greg's fingers. Greg clenched his fist so tightly that his biceps bulged and his face became red in effort. He watched and felt as the destroyed nuts were mushed further and further, oozing between his fingers and dripping to the floor. The sight was too much and Greg explosively came, coating the inside of his slacks with ropes of jizz he could feel running down his leg.

With a quick twist of his wrist, Greg pulled his still closed fist away from the young man, ripping off his entire squashed scrotum in one quick motion. The screaming and writhing were at a fever pitch as Greg help up the bloody glob, which had mostly already dripped through his fingers, then proceeded to smear it all over the Latino's face.

"Great new moisturizer!"

"It really does wonders for the skin!"

The businessmen cat called as the now passed out stud stood suspended on the pole, his face dripping with the innards of his nuts.

Then there was just one pair to destroy.

The last young man, a burly, bearish red head with meaty oblong testicles was beyond hysterics. He was attempting to close his legs so hard that for a moment it looked as though he may actually be successful, though the same men in black who had secured him stood silently in the background ready to restrain him if he did.

"Hmm.. a fire crotch. What oh what shall we do with these..." Greg mused, giving the boy's nuts a slap with his gloved hand.

SQUISH!

Although there was virtually no effort on Greg's part, the red head's right nut instantly burst from the blow.

"Damn it! I wasn't ready yet! You piece of shit! Lousy weak balls!"

Greg was enraged. Getting the chance to be the Crusher during Market Mash Up was a once in a lifetime chance, and here this prick was ruining his last moments to savior crushing testicles by having one blow apart at the slightest hit. Greg grabbed the now mushy right side of the sack and began to squeeze, splitting the sack open instantly and letting the mashed ball squirt out.

The red head's eyes rolled in horror and pain and he promptly passed out.

"Oh no you don't, fucking prick!"

Greg punched the boy in the face with his gloved hand shattering most of his teeth and breaking his jaw like glass. Several of the watching businessmen winced in feigned sympathy.

"Wake him up! Wake him up!" Greg shouted at the men in black, who came over and calmly administered smelling salts to the red head. They removed his gag so that he could spit out his shattered teeth and blood.

"Please! Please!" he wailed, though he knew it was hopeless.

Greg grabbed the left nut with the glove and was about to simply rip it off as he had done with the Latino but stopped. He had a better idea. He inserted his gloved finger into the hole made by the exploded right nut and began to rip and tear the remaining scrotum. The red head writhed and pleaded, screamed and begged, his head rolling in a desperate effort to pass out and escape the pain, but Greg kept instructing for the men in black to keep him awake with salts.

When the scrotum had been ripped to shreds, Greg removed the glove and placed it gently on the ground. He then knelt and examined the now totally exposed left nut with his bare hands. It was firm, large and a greyish-reddish color. Even the slightest touch to the sensitive, vulnerable organ made the red head scream in pain. Greg grabbed the orb in his bare hand and squeezed as hard as he could. Although such an action would have caused the red head's sex life to instantly explode had he been wearing the glove, Greg was annoyed to find that the organ resisted any deformation when using just his hand.

Greg then proceeded to place the red head's last, whole nut in one palm while pounding into it with this fist, hammering the rapidly swelling nut mercilessly. The red head's squeals were now inhuman sobs, which only helped arouse the crow even more, many of them had already creamed their pants from the nut bursting spectacle.

"Break damn thing..."

WHACK WHACK WHACK

"Break!' Greg shouted as he attempted to mush the poor nut with his bare hands.. but it didn't crack.

Greg continued pounding the nut until it eventually started to get softer, and softer ... and softer....

SQUICK.!

Though it wasn't nearly as explosive as when he had blown apart balls with the glove, the wet popping sound and satisfying, membrane crunching sensation told Greg that this red head bear wouldn't be siring anymore children.

Awake for his entire, slow castration the red head was mercilessly allowed to finally pass out.

Greg felt the nut in his hands, it had split open down the middle and was oozing nut guts.

"Look, just like a cracked nut."

The gathered executives laughed.

Greg took one final look back at the line of destroyed, nutless studs and thought to himself "This is a helluva lot better than a weekend at the office."

Activity 3: Golf

The air in the small, brightly lit room was chilly but not quite cold. Light bounced off three of the highly reflective steely gray walls. On the fourth was an enormous flat panel television, easily 70 inches on the diagonal, playing a test pattern. Cables hung lazily from the bottom of the television to the ground. On the floor directly in front of the screen was a chalk outline of a spread eagle body, with cuff like restraints where the arms and legs would be.

The silence of the room was broken as a dozen sharply dressed businessmen ranging from their early thirties to mid-sixties filed in, casually chatting about business and the weather. None of them were particularly impressed by the 'small' television displaying nothing, but a few of them did remark at the odd marking on the floor, wondering aloud what the point of it was. When they had all gathered, a handsome Asian gentleman in his thirties dressed entirely in black walked into the room and took a spot in front of the screen. The gathered men grew quiet, the titans of industry silenced in anticipation as if the most important person in the world was standing before them. The game had begun.

"Gentleman, welcome! I hope you've all been having a great time this weekend. But what would a weekend at a country club be without a round of golf..."

The confusion in the room was palpable.

"Bring him in," the announcer shouted calmly, ostensibly to no one.

No sooner had he given the command than two tall, broad shouldered men in black enter, their faces obscured by large mirror lens sun glasses. One of them got to work silently handing each of the businessmen a golf club, his stoic expression never wavering. Meanwhile, the other man in black was literally dragging a naked young man into position in front of the screen. The victim, a relatively short but powerfully built blonde in his mid-twenties had been bound and gagged, but was still managing to put up quite a fight, screaming loudly even through the gag. When he was in front of the screen, the man in black threw him to the ground and before the blonde could gain his bearings, the man in black who had been handing out golf clubs took the last one in his hands and proceeded to beat the young man into submission. The two men in black quickly got to work rolling the young man on his back, outstretching his arms and legs so that he was spread eagle, in the shape of the chalk outline, and shackled him to the floor. The blonde was starting to stir out of the daze of his beating in time to feel one of the men in black roughly grabbing his huge round testicles and banding them tightly in what felt to be athletic tape but it much stiffer. The man kept winding the tape around the base of the blonde man's sack until his large, round nuts were several inches from his body, the stiff binding making his balls stick up perpendicular to the ground, looking like two golf balls waiting on a tee.

The gathered men quickly began to realize what was about to happen, a few of them openly rubbing their swelling crotches at the prospect. One of the men in black, his job finished, abruptly left the room without saying a word. The other proceeded to attach two electrodes held by tape to each of the blonde's bulging testicles, then ran the attached wires and connected them to the apparently useless cables hanging from the television. As soon as he did so, the monitor came to life. Two large computer generated golf balls appeared on the screen against a black background. They were rotating slowly.

As soon as the last man in black left the room and closed the door, the announcer continued "This is Rupture Golf. The sensors attached to each of our man's balls is telling the system how round, or not, his golf balls are..."

The announcer knelt down between the muscular blonde's quivering legs and grabbed the enormous right nut in his hand. He squeezed, eliciting a squeal of pain from the trapped stud and, like clockwork the golf ball on the right side of the screen, while still rotating, started to change from while to pink. He held the pressure steadily, the animated golf ball corresponding to the blonde's right testicle turning more and more pink.

"See, the more damage you inflict, the more red it gets. The point of this golf game is to get the golf balls on the screen as red as possible."

The men chuckled.

The announcer loosened his grip on the doomed right nut and the golf ball on the screen slowly transitioned back to white. The men formed a line, their clubs at the ready.

"Whenever you're ready, gentleman."

The announcer had barely gotten out of the way before the first man cocked back his club and let it swing wildly into the tied 'golf balls' on the floor. The blonde squealed and tried desperately to close his legs, but he was constrained tightly to the floor. His large, round balls still perched helplessly aloof. As the club connected, both animated golf balls flashed red and, for a moment, the left ball stopped rotating. They were both still transitioning from red to pink when the next man took his spot.

The businessman took his time carefully lining up his aim, the crowd behind him cheering him on.

"Fore!" he shouted playfully as he sent the heavy wooden club sailing with a whoosh through the air.

It connected solidly with the left testicle. The left golf ball on the screen shook violently and flashed.

The third man, noticing that the left golf ball on the screen was still vibrating slightly and wasn't turning from red to white as quickly as the other, purposefully took aim at the poor blonde's left nut.

"I think I'm gonna' get a hole in one..." he joked mockingly, not breaking eye contact with crying stud as his club collided full force with his left testicle.

The golf ball on the left side of the screen rocked violently and flashed to burgundy. The ball on the right turned more red.

The fourth man took up position, lining up his club so that it would smack in the middle of the bound sack and swung the club so hard that, when it connected, the resultant shockwaves actually caused pain in his upper arm. The damage to the blonde's junk was equally devastating. To everyone's delight, an animated crack appeared down the middle of the right golf ball. The left was shaking and pulsing from blood red to dark burgundy.

"Uh oh. Doesn't look good for our friend," the announcer said mockingly. Everyone, except the blonde, laughed.

Amazingly the blonde was still conscious for the fifth and sixth hits. By now the golf ball on the right side of the screen had split into two pieces and the one on the left had developed a large crack. They were now both dark burgundy. No longer fading back toward white.

"Look at how detailed the animation is," the seventh man remarked coolly, impressed at how life like the golf ball animation was.

"Fore!" with a whoosh his club sailed into the young man's swollen sack. There was a sickening, wet SPLAT as the golf ball on the left exploded into four pieces. The one of the right shook violently and began to crumble into chunks.

"My turn!" the eighth man laughed, taking a casual golf stance. By now the blonde's sack was a swollen mass, the once obvious outline of two balls was starting to disappear.

WHOOSH!

POP! The animated golf balls both shattered into multiple pieces. The computer was now rendering them not as solid objects, but as gooey masses that were starting to 'drip' and 'ooze' on the screen. The men laughed and pointed.

"Did you hear that? It actually went 'pop'" said one of the onlookers. Indeed, the blonde's right nut had exploded with an almost comical sloshing 'POP' sound.

The ninth man took his spot. He wanted to be sure to do the most damaged, so lined up his shot carefully, grabbing the club firmly with both hands.

WHOOSH! SPLAT!

The image on the screen looked less and less like two broken golf balls and more like two piles of red goop.

The tenth man wasted no time, swinging wildly into the deflating sack. There were now just two piles of mushy goop showing on the screen.

"I think we broke them,"

Everyone laughed.

"I still get a shot!" came the eleventh golfer as he took his spot.

He had just let his club sail toward the purple, mushy mass between the blonde's legs, stopping just before the head of his club connected.

"I have an idea, Jon, come up here."

Jon, the twelfth and final golfer, a tall attractive man in his forties, stood next to the eleventh golfer.

The on looking group looked on curiously as Jon and the other man whispered amongst themselves, clearly coordinating a finishing finale to the blonde's sex life.

"Okay, let's do it,"

The two stood on either side of the doomed sack and raised their clubs. They were going to slam their clubs into each other, with the blonde's sack being mashed in between.

"Three... two... one..."

"FORE!" everyone shouted at once as the two clubs sailed toward each other.

The pulpy mass was viciously crushed between the two golf club heads, which were practically touching the contents had been so liquefied. And before anyone thought anything of it, the clubs were retracted...

"Three... two... one... FORE!"

The clubs again slammed into each other, only this time they connected completely. The blonde, who had long since passed out, shot his head up and let out a guttural scream as his assaulted nut sack burst open, splattering the two men standing over him with the gooey remains of his once truly enormous testicles. The golf balls on the monitor, now looked to be nothing more than piles of unrecognizable goop.

The two golfers toss down their clubs, making sure the goo covered heads landed on the blonde's face. They gave each other triumphant high fives as they joined the others.

Without prompting, the door of the room opened and the two men in black from early swooped in, quickly uniting the passed out young man and carrying him out of the room. The gathered businessmen looked on, almost in pity, as the desexed muscular jock was carried off.

The announcer again took this spot in front of the room as the door closed behind the men in black.

"Well, gentleman. I'm glad you enjoyed that practice round. Let's see if we can't get a hole in one on the next go,"

Again, demonstrating the amazing choreography of the whole affair, the door opened right on cue, the men in black again carrying in a bound and gagged man. A strikingly good looking, olive skinned Italian in his early thirties, with rippling muscles and enormous, swinging nuts dangling between his tree trunk legs. As he was being restrained to the ground, the second man in black began exchanging the golf clubs from the first round with croquet mallets with heads so heavy some of the businessmen -- none of them particularly frail -- had difficultly holding them up.

When the two men in black left, the first golfer took his position between the doomed Italian's muscular legs. The animated goofballs had returned to the screen, white and pristine.

The Italian, begging and sobbing through his gag could lift his head just far enough to look down over his rippled chest at his huge balls perched straight up in the constraints. His eyes bugged out and he struggled futilely against his restraints as he saw the first heavy mallet being lined up. The businessman holding it, a tall man in his forties, was clearly struggling to control the bottom-heavy mallet... this was going to be quite an impact...

WHOOSH!

The Italian screamed into his gag so loud even the businessman who had just took a swing look startled. But it was too late. The animated golf balls on the screen were both instantly turned to animated piles of red goop. There was a vicious, wet double SPLAT as the mallet head collided with - and blew apart - the huge Italian bollocks in a single blow. The Italian's eyes rolled as he watched a gooey mixture splatter all over his washboard stomach.

"Oops!" the businessman laughed derisively.

"Bring in the next one," the Italian heard the announcer shout out before mercifully passing out.

Activity 4: The Banquet

The large, cavernous interior of the Country Club pole barn had been totally transformed into a posh banquet hall. Delicate white and canary yellow bolts of silk fabric were suspended from ornate Corinthian columns to give the vaulted ceilings a softer depth. The concrete floor had been covered over in white marble tiles. A string quartet of men dressed all in black played softly in the corner, their music combined with the glow of huge candelabras giving the banquet hall an air of sophistication. Evenly spaced throughout the hall were five large, semi circular tables draped in red fabric, a black column bolted to the floor at each table. The place settings complete with fine china dishes with platinum accents and solid silver flatware. The water goblets were Italian crystal. Indeed, the whole setup was so refined that the fifty gathered businessmen, ten per table, hardly seemed to notice - or care -- that the atmosphere was in stark contrast of what was about to happen there.

When everyone was settled, the string quartet fell silent and an announcer, dressed entirely in black with slicked black hair, took to the middle of the room and began to speak.

"Good evening, gentleman. I hope everyone enjoyed this year's Rupture Fest,"

The crowd broke into riotous applause.

"As always, we are going to be dispatching of the last... candidates... in our annual banquet."

The announcer had barely finished his statement when five men in black suits emerged from the sides of the venue, each roughly escorting a naked bound and gagged young man. The captive men ranged from their early twenties to late thirties, and covered a range of body types and races, but the thing each had in common was a large, dangling pair of testicles swinging helplessly between his legs. The men were struggling fruitlessly as the men in black effortlessly lead each one to a table and shackled them tightly to the black column. Their arms were tied behind their backs and their ankles were shackled to the bottom of the column in such a manner that the men couldn't close their legs.

They were all trapped, legs spread wide, balls swinging in full view of the ten men gathered around their respective tables. When the men were all secured, the men in black silently left the room, replaced almost immediately by ten men in white chef's uniforms. The ten chefs were all wheeling in small wooden prep carts, the tops were filled with a variety of knives, tenderizing mallets, seasons and other cooking paraphernalia. Some of the chef's carts had hot plates. Some had open flame burners. One of the carts had a black box the size of a large microwave oven, but its function was not immediately clear. The chefs took their stations, one per table, in front of the bound men, and quickly got to work setting up their work stations. The gathered executives licked their lips and asked questions casually about the mallets and knives and what the chefs were planning on doing with the huge nuts offered up for the banquet.

At the first table, a Latin man in his mid twenties with heavy, firm balls the size of eggs that hung a few inches from his body was struggling valiantly against his bonds. He was tall, with perfectly tanned skin and well defined but not overwhelming muscles, his shoulder length black hair was styled carefully to frame his handsome face. Despite his struggling, the black column didn't budge. Instead, his efforts only made his large bollocks swing wildly between his legs. His cock, totally limp, was quite thick but only a small nub against the base of his balls. The chef readied a hot plate directly under the dangling sack and placed a large cast iron frying pan on it. He turned on the plate and applied a small amount of extra virgin olive oil to it with a brush. After a few moments, he held a hand over the pan, nodded in approval and turned to address the businessmen.

"At this table we're going to be making scrambled eggs," he said laughing.

The gathered executives, all of them growing hard in their designer suits, nodded in approval.

Meanwhile, the heat wafting up from the plate several inches below the base of his sack was starting to heat up the Latino's balls. Beads of sweat formed all along the length of his scrotum, and the heavy balls sank further in their sack from the heat.

"First, we need to thoroughly scramble the eggs," said the chef picking up a spatula.

He began brutally beating the Latin man's sack like an overstuffed piñata. He screamed into his gag as his defenseless nuts were batted with blow after blow, bouncing wildly in a vain attempt to escape. The chef was raining down blow after devastating blow, purplish welts and bruises were appearing all over the once pristine scrotal skin. After ten minutes of non stop pounding, the chef calmly put down the spatula and examined the now swollen, red nuts with his hands.

"Hmm.. not quite scrambled. With hard eggs like this, I sometimes use something a bit harder."

The chef reached for a wooden mallet with a large head and started hitting the Latin's left nut repeatedly. The entire sack bounced as the left ball was thoroughly mashed in the sack. The Latin was sobbing and rolling his head back as half of his man hood was being pulverized. The chef was drawing his arm back as far as he could each time before striking the nut.

THUMP! THUMP! THUMP! THUMP!

The chef continued this for several minutes before changing his focus to the right nut...

THUMP! THUMP! THUMP! THUMP!

The man's balls were swelling and the impact sounds were getting softer and wetter. The chef set down the mallet and again examined the man's eggs, rolling them roughly in the sack.

"Hmm.. they're starting to crack," the chef said smiling letting go of the beet red sack, "This should do it,"

The chef reached for an immersion blender and turned it on. The plastic blades whirred to live, spinning so fast it looked like a blur. The chef moved the blades with deliberate slowness toward the hanging sack and the Latin's eyes bugged out in anticipation.

"See, I've dulled the blades on this model, we wouldn't want to cut the eggs, so they'll just beat them until they crack in their shell."

As he spoke the blades made contact with the bulging left nut. The Latin stud threw his head back and screamed, though it was barely audible through the gag. Spinning at hundreds of revolutions per minute, the blades beat relentless into the quickly swelling, bruising organ. He then moved to the right, then the left. The chef alternated which nut was beaten for nearly ten minutes. By then it was obvious that the man's balls had ruptured. He had long since passed out, by the time the chef put the blender down and again reached for the clearly deflating organs.

"Mmm, almost there."

He picked up two wooden mallets and positioned one on each side of the man's sack, then slammed them together.

SPLAT! SPLAT! SPLAT!

The Latin sack was now totally flat, filled with nothing but mush. The chef put down the mallets an again examined his eggs. The contents were thoroughly scrambled, just a few small chunks could be felt through the mush. Without a word, the chef diced tomatoes, shredded cheese and mixed spices, adding them into the pan. He then reached for a large knife and, in one swoop sliced through the bottom of the man's sack. The Latino groaned slightly as the chef proceeded to grab the top of the sack and squeeze downward, squeezing out the gooey innards like chunky salsa. The remains of the bull nuts landed with wet splats into the pan, where they were quickly mixed with the other ingredients. When the gooey mass had cooked thoroughly, the chef removed the omelet from the pan onto a serving plate adorned with parsley sprigs.

"Those were some rather large eggs," he joked as he looked as the enormous nut omelet. He portioned it up and served it to the ten waiting executives.

Meanwhile, at the second table a short, lanky man in his late twenties with shaggy blonde hair was awaiting his fate. Between his then legs two truly enormous testicles hung several inches from his body. The young man had boyishly good looks, and gorgeous deep blue eyes. His vaguely defined abs were tensing intensely from fear and panic.

The chef at this table had brought a large, clear pot of water to rolling boil immediately under the hanging sack and was casually dicing carrots, onions and other vegetables into the water. He was casually sprinkling in salt as he spoke.

"Today I'm going to be making a nut soup for you,"

The executives at the table applauded politely; the young captive struggled and cried.

"First, we need to thoroughly boil the nuts to firm up the insides."

Without ceremony, the chef pressed a button on his prep table and the black column that was holding up the blonde began to lower into the ground. The blonde screamed as he was forced into a squatting position. His dangling nuts inched closer, and closer, and closer to the boiling liquid until they just breached the rolling surface.

The entire bloated sack turned instantly red and the blonde's eyes grew wide and he passed out. He continued to be lowered until his balls were totally submerged, then the column stopped lowering. The blonde man was now squatting, his large nuts totally covered in boiling water, visible through the transparent glass. The executives took sick pleasure peering into the pot and watching the balls turn blood red, bobbling slightly in the rolling bubbles.

"How long do you boil them?" one of them asked casually after five minutes.

"Just a bit longer..." The chef answered as he calmly mixed together beef broth in a nearby bowl.

As he continued to prep the rest of the ingredients for his soup, the blonde's balls, now swollen to bursting, were fiery red, blisters were appearing all over the scrotum, but the balls inside looked to be getting more firm. The chef looked into the water and nodded in approval. He reached for a spoon and jammed it into the pot, striking the boy's right nut viciously. Through the clear pot, the impact was clearly visible, the spoon colliding with the now cooked, tough nut with a thud.

"Ah, they're ready." the chef said, putting down the spoon and reaching for a butcher knife.

The executives leaned in, breathless in anticipation, when the chef stopped the knife in mid swing.

"Oops, almost forgot something,"

He turned on a second hot plate and picked up a large flat branding iron with his free hand. He warmed it until it was glowing red. He then lopped off the blonde man's balls at the base and quickly pushed the brand into the gaping hole, sealing it and stopping too much blood from entering the water. The men watched as the heavy round balls sank to the bottom, and then were bobbled to the top by the rolling liquid.

"Now we blend,"

The chef grabbed a large blender and put it into the pot. At first, the huge red ball sack simply spun around the resultant vortex. The chef repositioned it slightly and grinned cruelly as the balls were snagged by the whirling blades. The bloated sack was sliced cleanly in two, and as the chef expected, they were now totally firm. It looked like a large piece of meat had been split in half, not gooey, mashed nuts. As the blender continued, the balls were pulverized further, bursting into meaty chunks. When he was satisfied, he poured in the beef broth and a few spices, blended the soup further - totally turning the tough nuts into small chunks-- then ladled the steaming hot mixture out to the gathered executives.

"Bon apetit!" he said, as the men slurped down the rich, flavorful nut soup.

At the third table, a beefy red headed man in his early thirties with scruffy facial hair was sobbing and trying to beg for mercy through his gag. He had powerful, muscular arms and powerful tree trunk like legs and thighs, his well-defined, if a bit pudgy stomach eas heaving as he breathed. Despite himself, his cock was fully erect, protruding nearly nine inches from his body, the thick organ culminating in a mushroom head. His pendulous nuts, oblong golf ball sized things, had been shaved clean. The gathered executives couldn't help but be impressed by the sheer size of them.

"I think we're going to get full!" one of them joked.

The chef turned on a flaming burner just inches from the doomed balls and began,

"Today, we're just going to be doing an old fashioned nut roast,"

.

He then rose the burner so that the top of the flame was literally a quarter inch from the man's large balls. The red head was screaming horribly, blisters appearing on his nuts and cock shaft.

"I like mine barbequed," the chef said applying a thick coating of barbeque sauce over the roasting ball sack and over the entire length of the man's cock. The red head's cock stayed hard, pulsing with each heart beat as his nuts were slowly boiled in their sack. After a few minutes, the chef looked at the sack, the right side starting to bulge, and rolled his eyes.

"This sometimes happens, usually the sack splits when heated this long, releasing the steam. But sometimes it doesn't, so it builds up until..."

POP!

As if on cue the man's right nut suddenly exploded violently, spraying some of the executives with hot nut meat. The red head looked down in horror before passing out.

"Damn, what a waste of a meaty nut. Oh well," the chef said coolly as he watched the remaining nut be roasted.

"For the last part, I usually remove them..."

He picked up a long, sharp rod, about six inches long and rammed it into the man's mushroom head, impaling the still hard organ. He then took a butcher knife and sliced off the red headed stud's entire sexual package at the base. He motioned for a man in black to come to the table, he quickly removed the bleeding red head, getting him out of the way. The chef then held the man's last nut, via the rod sticking out of his cock, rotating it slowly over the flame until both the nutsack and the cock were charred black.

He placed the large meaty cock and thoroughly roasted nut on a serving plate, dicing it into ten pieces, applying more sauce and giving one bite sized piece each to the executives.

"Mmm, this was meaty," one of the executives remarked finishing his section of the man's ball before feasting on the charred wedge of cock he'd been served.

Meanwhile at the fourth table, a powerfully built black man in his twenties was struggling against his bounds. His large, almost perfectly round nuts were stretched several inches from his body by rubber rings. They were dangling above a microwave-oven sized black box. The gathered executives were openly confused by what they were seeing.

"At this table, we'll be making dessert. Testicle and vanilla bean ice cream,"

Some of the men licked their lips.

"First, I like to soften the testicles to release the flavor,"

The chef took two heavy mallets, and positioned them on either side of the nuts bulging at the bottom of the sack...

SPLAT! SPLAT!

The chef slammed the mallets together as hard as he could, squashing the firm black nuts between the mallet heads. The executives thought the man's balls were going to burst....

SPLAT! SPLAT! SPLOSH!

The man writhed and screamed into his gag as the chef brutally flattened his sack. By the tenth blow, it was obvious the man's left nut had totally ruptured, that side of the sack mushy and lumpy.

"That should do it," said the chef putting down his mallets.

He then pushed a button on his table that lowered the man until he was in a squatting position. His sack was now resting directly on top of the black box.

"This is a blast chiller," the chef explained, "We use it in the kitchen when we have to instantly freeze ice into water, and things like that."

He opened a small round door at the top of this specially made blast chiller and stuffed the man's half mashed sack inside. He then closed the opening as tightly as he could around the sack and pressed a button. The man let out a howl of agony and passed out. The machine whirred quietly as the chef proceeded to produce pre-made vanilla ice cream in a large bowl, blending in a few other ingredients like heavy cream and mint while he waited for the machine to finish. There was a ding, and the door opened. The cycle was done.

The chef pulled the man's balls out of the machine, his large black balls covered in frost. The sack as hard as a rock. With his knife, he sliced the balls at the base and motioned for a man in black to remove the nutted stud lest he bleed all over the pristine white ice cream. The chef handed the frozen balls to the executive on the far side of the semi circle.

"Feel it, pass it around,"

The men took delight fondling the rock hard, cold sex organs in their hands, remarking on their size and how perfectly preserved the blast chilling had left them.

When the chef had the balls again, he proceeded to coat them in chocolate syrup, then put them on the table top where he proceeded to pound them with the same mallet he had used earlier. The severed, frozen organs shattered like glass as the chef continued to beat and bound them into frozen chunks of testicle. He then scooped the chocolate, crushed nuts and mixed them into the ice cream.

"Enjoy!" he said smiling as he handed the ten executives their vanilla ice cream with chocolate nuts.

Elsewhere, at the last table a gorgeous, svelte Italian man with chiseled facial features outlined by his black hair, was awaiting his fate. He wasn't the largest of the men, but was clearly the best defined. His abs were like a washboard. His biceps and pecs were clearly taught. His legs were perfectly sculpted. And between his legs two of the largest testicles of that year's event were tightly held against his body. The executives were amazed at the sheer size of his balls. They were large even compared to the others they had seen -- and flattened.

"At this table, we're going to be making a classic. Mashed Testicles with butter."

The chef wasted no time roughly grabbing the Italian's meaty balls and pulling them forward to the prep table. The Italian screamed as the chef tightly bound the sack with tape, trapping them several inches from his body onto the table. They bulged obscenely against the skin, veins clearly visible.

"The other chefs get a little elaborate with their preparation but I like to take it back to basics."

The chef produced a very large metal mallet used for tenderizing steaks, rose it over the enormous left testicle and sent it down.

SPLAT!

The Italian's head threw back as he hollered into his gag.

SPLAT! SPLAT! SPLAT!

The chef's face was red from effort as he laid waste to the huge ball. It didn't take too many blows before the left nut totally collapsed, quite suddenly, like a balloon that had popped

SPLOSH!

"That's one down," the chef remarked and immediately go to work on the last nut.

SPLAT! SPLAT! SPLAT!

Amazingly the Italian was still conscious, looking down in terror as he watched his ridiculously large nut pounded over and over until...

SPLOOOOOOOSH!

There was a loud wet sound as his testicle ruptured under the mallet's assault. The Italian finally passed out as the chef reached for a slightly smaller wooden mallet.

"Now we just beat until smooth,"

"Yeah, make sure to get all the lumps out," one of the executives joked.

SPLAT! SPLOSH! SPLAT! SPLAT!

The chef brought the mallet down dozens of time, being sure to strike every inch of the now totally flat sack. The enormous scrotum was now flattened to a quarter inch, no sign they had ever been filled with testicles that were each almost twice as large as eggs.

"Now we just mixed them in with butter, heat and serve."

The chef sliced into the scrotum right at the seam and squeezed until the nut goop inside was in a large bowl. The sheer volume of goo in the bowl was a testament to how large this Italian's nuts had been. The chef then casually mixed in butter and herbs, put the mixture into a pot on his hot plate and cooked until the smell of burning meat was evident.

"Enjoy!" he said as he scooped the mixture, with a consistency of corned beef, into ten waiting bowls for the executives.

When everyone was done, wait staff cleared the dishes and set down another course for the executives, this time consisting of much more traditional giant lobster tails and steaks. As the men dined, chatting causally about business, ten more attractive, muscular hunks, ranging in age from early to late twenties were lead. They were stripped naked and were chained to each other at the ankles. Their powerful arms tied behind their backs and their mouths gagged. Each man's huge nuts were swinging defenselessly between their legs.

"No need to stop enjoying your dinner," came an announcer, "We thought you'd enjoy some dinner entertainment."

The executives leaned in, eye fucking and examining the muscular, helpless young men

.

"There aren't enough to go around, but if you haven't personally gotten to mash a pair this weekend, step right up and take your pick." the announcer instructed.

Meanwhile a man in black wheeled out a cart with knives, mallets, hammers, large fireworks, lighters, pliers and other instruments of nut torture and placed it in front of the ten hysterical men.

"Oh, I'll go," an executive in his late forties said wiping his mouth and standing from his table.

He approached the table and grabbed a wood working clamp, usually used to hold pieces of wood together while glue was drying. The clamp had a squeeze trigger, that got tighter as the user pumped it with his hand. He carefully positioned the right nut of a sobbing, muscular Asian in his early twenties and pumped the trigger as fast as he could. He didn't break eye contact with the large nut as it flattened between the clamp plates, the flattening organ bulge between the clamps, dimpled, got flatter...

SPLOSH!

The young man's nut burst open as it collapsed under the pressure. The front of the businessman's slacks were slick with precum as he quickly opened the clamp and placed it over the man's last nut...

Meanwhile, another executive had taken position in front of a relatively short, sandy haired blonde with rippling abs and oblong, large testicles. He slowly skewered the organs, as the victim writhed and screamed, with long, thick metal rods. When he had shoved three of them completely through the man's testicles he slowly retracted them. The man was barely conscious to feel the executive finish off his organs with a mallet.

The brutal destruction of the remaining sacks rounded out the evening. Balls were flattened in vices, blown into shredded gore with fireworks, roasted into charred husks with burners, crushed and mangled by hand and splattered into goop with heavy mallets. By the end of it there was literally nothing resembling a whole testicle among the line of men. As they were dragged out of the banquet hall, the announcer took his place in the center of the venue and declared.

"Now that was an amazing Rupture Fest! See you all next year."

Made in the USA
Middletown, DE
24 July 2022

69962510R00050